STAR WARS® INFINITIES

THE EMPIRE STRIKES BACK

STAR WARS® INFINITIES

THE EMPIRE STRIKES BACK

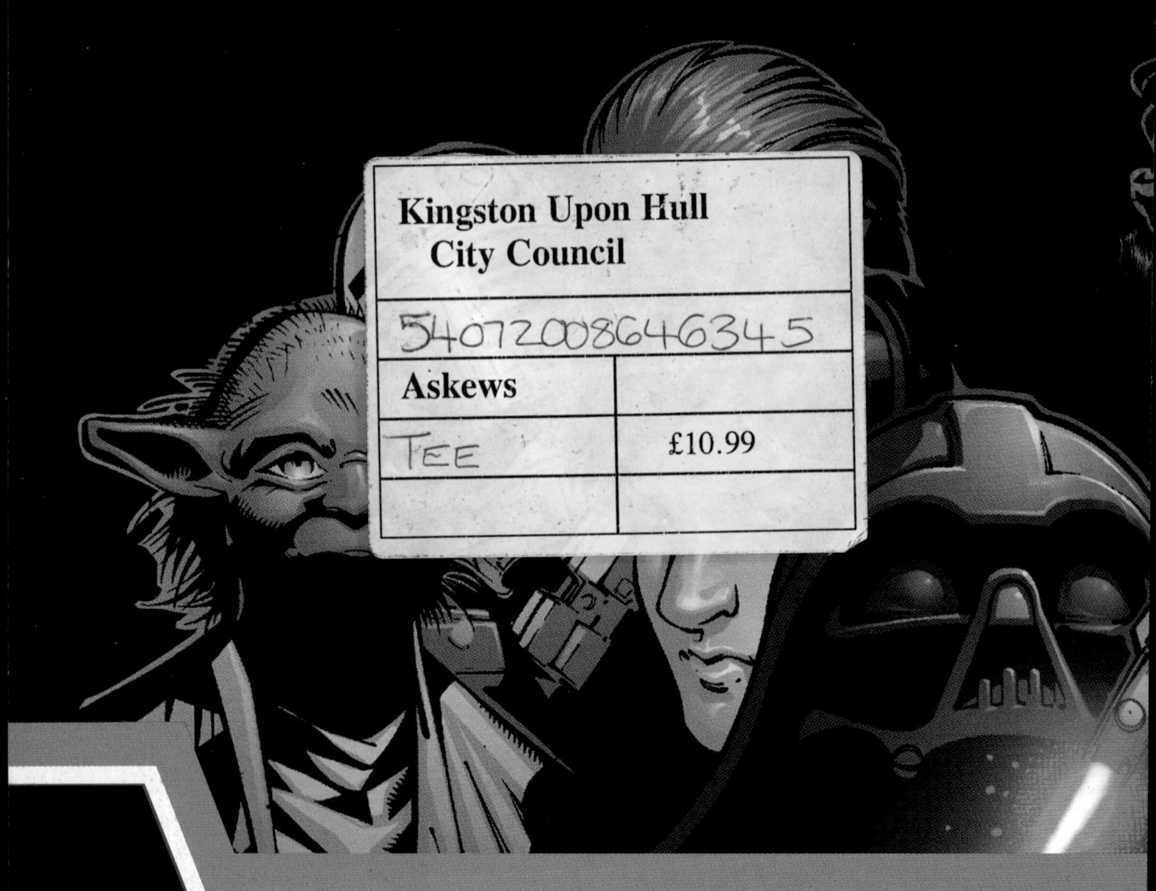

script DAVE LAND

pencils DAVIDÉ FABBRI

inks CHRISTIAN DALLA VECCHIA

colors DAN JACKSON

letters STEVE DUTRO

cover pencils CHRIS BACHALO

cover inks TIM TOWNSEND

DARK HORSE BOOKS™

publisher MIKE RICHARDSON

collection designers KEITH WOOD & DARIN FABRICK

art director MARK COX

assistant editor PHILIP SIMON

editors RANDY STRADLEY & PHIL AMARA

SPECIAL THANKS TO CHRIS CERASI AND LUCY AUTREY WILSON AT LUCAS LICENSING

Star Wars®: Infinities—THE EMPIRE STRIKES BACK

This volume collects issues one through four of the Dark Horse comic-book series *Star Wars®: Infinities—The Empire Strikes Back.*

Dark Horse Books
A division of Dark Horse Comics, Inc.
10956 SE Main Street
Milwaukie, OR 97222

darkhorse.com starwars.com

To locate a comic-shop in your area, call the Comic Shop Locator Service toll free at (888) 266-4226.

First edition: February 2003
ISBN-10: 1-56971-904-7 ISBN-13: 978-1-56971-904-6

10 9 8 7 6 5 4 3

Printed in China

A LONG TIME AGO, IN A GALAXY FAR, FAR AWAY . . . .

You know the story. Everybody knows the story. But what if the story changed—even just a little? What would happen to the characters? What would happen to the *Star Wars* galaxy?

Within the "Expanded Universe"—the novels, short stories, radio dramas, and graphic novels that cover the continuing (or untold) adventures of the *Star Wars* cast of characters—the continuity established in the films is strictly adhered to. The events in the motion pictures are the canon law to which every author must bow.

But within the *Infinities* line, those laws exist to be broken . . . carefully, and one at a time.

The rules are actually very simple: take the events and characters from one of the classic *Star Wars* films, throw in one happenstance, mishap, or technical glitch beyond the characters' control, and watch how that changes everything. In Dark Horse's first foray into *Infinities* (*A New Hope*), Luke Skywalker's valiant torpedo attack on the Death Star failed due to a faulty detonator—an event no one could have foreseen—and the Rebellion was dealt a debilitating setback.

In *Infinities—The Empire Strikes Back*, the fates once again conspire against Luke and his companions. But see for yourself . . .

EASY GIRL. WHAT IS IT? YOU SMELL SOMETHING?
WAAAAG! BWAAAG!
ON THE DESOLATE ICE PLANET OF HOTH, REBEL COMMANDER LUKE SKYWALKER PATROLS THE FROZEN TUNDRA, ON THE LOOKOUT FOR SIGNS OF AN IMPERIAL INVASION. LITTLE DOES HE KNOW THAT HIS PROBLEMS ARE MORE IMMEDIATE AND... PRIMAL. FURTHER, SKYWALKER COULD NOT BE AWARE OF HOW ONE INSTANT--ONE VARIATION IN A RANDOM SCENARIO--WILL RIPPLE FORWARD THROUGH TIME WITH STARTLING EFFECTS...

WAHHH!
SNAP

WHUMP

RRRRR!

FWAP
RRAAAH!

ECHO BASE.
HAN! HAN!
YES, YOUR HIGHNESS?
I THOUGHT YOU DECIDED TO STAY.

WELL, THE BOUNTY HUNTER WE RAN INTO ON ORD MANTELL CHANGED MY MIND.

HAN, WE NEED YOU!
WE?

"WHAT ABOUT WHAT YOU NEED?"

SHK

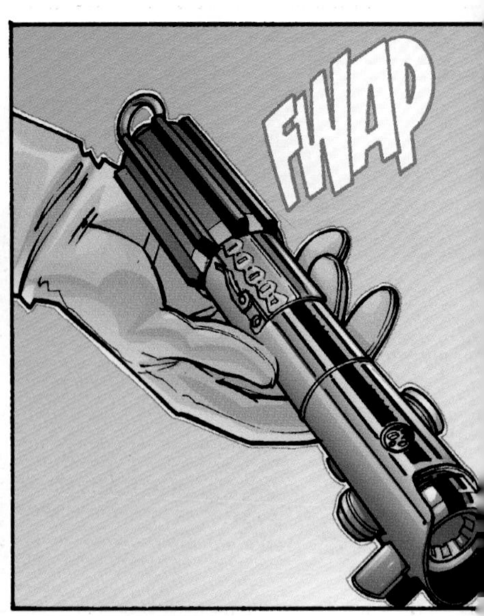
FWAP

RRRR!

KKRKK
UMM

RAAAH!

WRAAGH
VMMM
AAROOO

ARROOO!

FWMP
LUKE...
LUKE...

?!

GO TO THE DAGOBAH SYSTEM AND LEARN FROM YODA, THE JEDI MASTER WHO INSTRUCTED ME.
Ben...

Ben.

Ben.
LUKE!
I WOULD'VE BEEN HERE SOONER, BUT MY TAUNTAUN DIED!
HANG ON, KID.
Dagobah system... must go to Dagobah.
Find Master Yoda... train as Jedi...
JEDI?!
...Ben, he told me...
LUKE! DON'T DO THIS, BUDDY!
COME ON, GIVE ME A SIGN HERE!

YOU! MUST GO TO DAGOBAH!

COMMANDER SKYWALKER, DO YOU COPY? THIS IS ROGUE TWO.
ROGUE TWO, THIS IS COMMANDER SOLO. COME IN, ROGUE TWO...
COMMANDER SOLO, I READ YOU LOUD AND CLEAR. ARE YOU OKAY, COMMANDER?

AFFIRMATIVE, ROGUE TWO. BUT LUKE... LUKE IS DEAD.

LATER...
...SKYWALKER WAS LOVED BY ALL THOSE WHO KNEW HIM, AND HIS CONTRIBUTIONS TO THE FIGHT AGAINST GALACTIC TYRANNY WERE WITHOUT MEASURE.
HE WILL BE SORELY MISSED.

I'M SORRY, LEIA. I DID EVERY-THING I COULD...
BETWEEN HIS WOUNDS AND THE COLD... MAYBE IF I'D FOUND HIM SOONER...

IT'S NOT YOUR FAULT, HAN. YOU SAID HE TOLD YOU SOMETHING BEFORE HE DIED. WHAT WAS IT?

I'M SUPPOSED TO GO TO DAGOBAH AND FIND SOME-ONE NAMED YODA...
HE TOLD ME I'M SUPPOSED TO TRAIN TO BE A JEDI.

YOU? TRAIN AS A JEDI?
THOSE WERE HIS DYING WORDS.

VROOO
WHAT THE--?!
THE EMPIRE! THEY'VE FOUND US!
CHEWIE! FIRE 'ER UP! WE'RE GETTIN' OUT OF HERE!
MWARG! GRARPH!
WELL, PUT IT BACK ON!
THAT PROBE DROID COMMANDER SOLO RAN INTO EARLIER DEFINITELY BELONGED TO THE EMPIRE.
STAR DESTROYERS ARE IN ORBIT AND IMPERIAL WALKERS AND TIES ARE ALREADY PLANETSIDE.
BEGIN EVACUATION. SCRAMBLE THE SNOW-SPEEDERS.
IF THEY REACH THE POWER GENERATOR, WE'RE FINISHED.

LORD VADER, WE WERE ABLE TO BRING A SQUADRON OF TIE FIGHTERS IN UNDER THE REBEL SHIELD.
RESISTANCE WILL BE MINIMAL AND THE SHIELD WILL BE DOWN MOMENTARILY. YOU MAY START YOUR LANDING.
JANSON, AVOID THOSE TIES. THEY DON'T HAVE THE FIRE POWER TO TAKE OUT THE GENERATOR. CONCENTRATE ON THE WALKERS.
SURE THING, WEDGE.
WEDGE!

FVOOM
AGHH!

TARGET THE POWER GENERATOR. FIRE WHEN READY.

VEEOWW
VTT
VTT

THE GENERATOR IS DOWN! LAUNCH ALL TRANSPORTS IMMEDIATELY!
WHAT ABOUT THOSE STAR DESTROYERS?!
WE'LL HAVE TO HOPE OUR ESCORTS CAN KEEP THEM BUSY UNTIL THE TRANS-PORTS ENTER HYPERSPACE!

COME ON, LEIA. WE'RE LEAVING... NOW!
GOOD LUCK, GENERAL.

WAIT FOR ME!

TOOM

BTEW

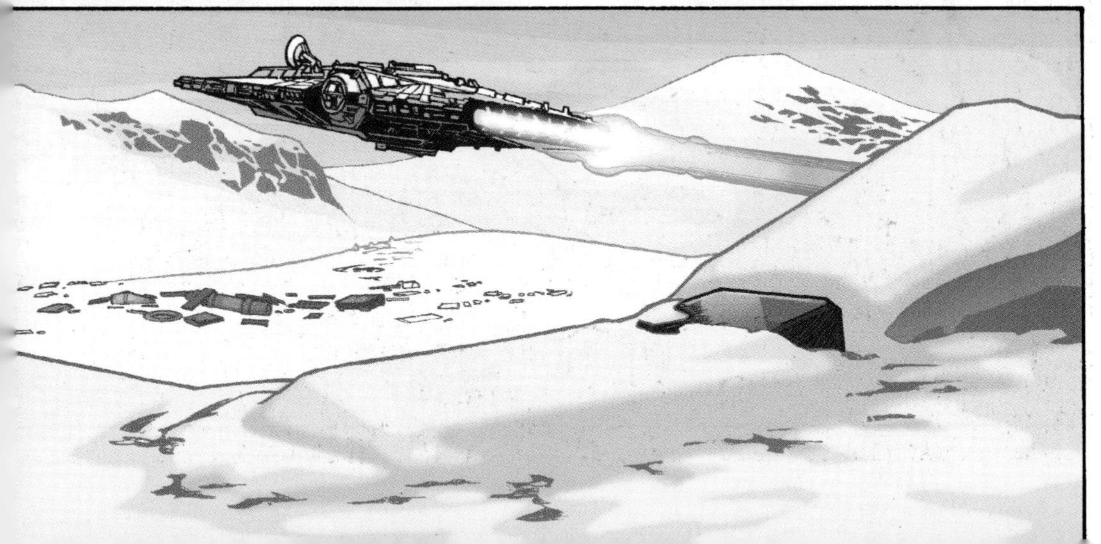

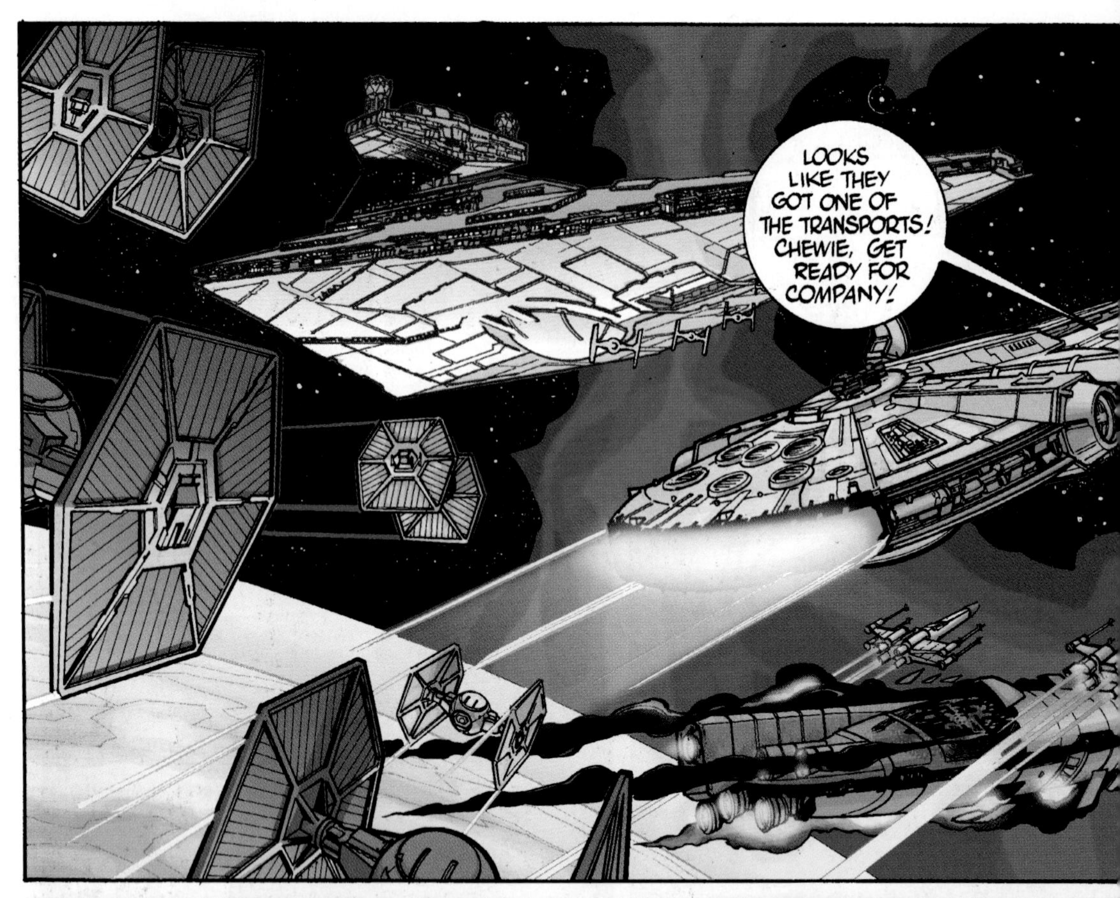
LOOKS LIKE THEY GOT ONE OF THE TRANSPORTS! CHEWIE, GET READY FOR COMPANY!

THOOM
VTT
VTT
HAN, DO SOMETHING!

WHAT DOES IT LOOK LIKE I'M DOING?!
NOT ENOUGH, THAT'S FOR SURE!
WELL, EXCUSE ME, YOUR HIGHNESS!
MAYBE YOU'D LIKE IT BETTER IF I FLEW INTO AN ASTEROID FIELD AND FOUND SOME COZY CAVE TO HIDE IN!
THAT'D BE A START!
THAT'S IT... HOLD ON, SWEET-HEART!
IT'S HEADED RIGHT FOR US!

CAPTAIN, THE SHIP'S DISAPPEARED FROM OUR SCOPES! THERE'S NO TRACE OF THEM!
THEY MUST HAVE JUMPED TO HYPERSPACE. RECALL THE REMAINING TIES AND LAY IN A PURSUIT COURSE FOR THE REBEL TRANSPORTS.
YOU NEVER FAIL TO SURPRISE ME, HAN SOLO...
SOMETIMES I SURPRISE MYSELF. WE'LL DETATCH AND FLOAT AWAY WITH THE SHIP'S GARBAGE BEFORE THEY ENTER HYPERSPACE.
THEN HEAD TO DAGOBAH? FOR LUKE...
I GUESS IT COULDN'T HURT.
NOT THAT I BUY INTO ANY OF THAT JEDI STUFF.
BUT, WE'LL NEVER MAKE IT TO DAGOBAH WITHOUT A HYPERDRIVE.
IS THERE SOMEWHERE WE CAN MAKE REPAIRS?
I'VE GOT A FRIEND, LANDO CALRISSIAN, HE RUNS A GAS MINE BETWEEN HERE AND DAGOBAH. HE'LL HELP US... I THINK.

CLOUD CITY, BESPIN...

HAN SOLO! YOU HAVE SOME NERVE SHOWING YOUR FACE AROUND HERE...

WHOA! WAIT A SEC! A LOT HAS CHANGED SINCE I LAST SAW YOU! I'M WITH THE REBELLION NOW.

THE REBELLION?! YOU?!
YEAH, I KNOW... ONE MINUTE I'M ON THE RUN FROM JABBA, AND THE NEXT THING I KNOW I'M FIGHTING THE EMPIRE.

ANY ENEMY OF THE EMPIRE IS A FRIEND OF MINE...
THANKS. WE'RE GOING TO NEED YOUR HELP.
THINGS HAVE BEEN PRETTY ROUGH LATELY. THE EMPIRE OVERRAN OUR BASE.
WE TOOK SOME HEAVY LOSSES AND... AND WE LOST A CLOSE FRIEND OF OURS--
YOU CAN STAY HERE AS LONG AS YOU NEED.
WE'LL ONLY STAY LONG ENOUGH TO GET THE FALCON FIXED, THEN WE'RE GONE.
SEE... I'M GOING TO TRAIN TO BE A JEDI KNIGHT.
YOU?! A JEDI? HA-HA!
GRAW AW AW!
THIS ISN'T FUNNY! LUKE DIED GIVING HAN THAT INFORMATION! FOR ALL WE KNOW, THE FATE OF THE REBELLION IS STANDING RIGHT HERE!

I'M SORRY, REALLY. IT'S JUST IF YOU KNEW HAN LIKE I DO, YOU'D FIND IT A LITTLE HARD TO SWALLOW.
I'LL GET MY BEST MECHANICS TO WORK ON THE FALCON RIGHT AWAY.

IF YOU'LL FOLLOW ME...

PLEASE MAKE YOURSELF COMFORTABLE, AND LET THE STAFF KNOW IF YOU NEED ANYTHING.
NOW IF YOU'LL EXCUSE ME, I HAVE ANOTHER GUEST WHO'S JUST ARRIVED. I'LL REJOIN YOU THIS EVENING.

HOW LONG HAS HE BEEN HERE?
HIS SHIP ARRIVED SHORTLY AFTER THE *MILLENNIUM FALCON* SET DOWN.

FWISH

WHAT ARE YOU DOING HERE?

LONG TIME NO SEE, LANDO.
I UNDERSTAND YOU HAVE SOMETHING I WANT.

FETT! WHAT ARE YOU DOING HERE?

SOLO. I KNOW HE'S HERE. MY EMPLOYER HAS UNFINISHED BUSINESS WITH HIM.
IT'S IN YOUR BEST INTERESTS TO COOP-ERATE.

YOU'VE GOT SOME NERVE, FETT!
AS THE ADMINISTRA-TOR OF THIS FACILITY, I SUGGEST YOU LEAVE BEFORE I HAVE YOU FORCIBLY REMOVED.

YOU MISUNDERSTAND. I'M NOT ASKING. I'M TELLING. MY EMPLOYER IS ON THE WAY HERE. YOU DON'T HAVE A CHOICE.

WHEN YOU PUT IT THAT WAY, IT MAKES A LOT MORE SENSE...
...I'VE NEVER BEEN ONE TO ARGUE WITH A BLASTER TO MY HEAD.

FOLLOW ME. I'LL TAKE YOU TO SOLO.

ONE FALSE MOVE, YOU'RE BOTH DEAD.

GRRAARGH!
HOOFF!
VTT
THUD

GIVE IT UP, FETT. THIS IS OVER. NOW!
DROP YOUR WEAPON.
DROP IT!
AGH!
FFFT
VTT

VOOSH
TOOM
Get off...get off...

URK!

WAM
GRAAGH!

ARE YOU ALL RIGHT?
YEAH. WONDERFUL.

IS HE DEAD?
NO. BUT HE WON'T BE GIVING US TROUBLE ANY TIME SOON.

DO YOU MIND TELLING ME WHAT THIS IS ALL ABOUT?
HE WAS HERE FOR YOU! SAID HIS EMPLOYER HAD SOME BUSINESS WITH YOU--!
JABBA!
THAT'S EXACTLY WHAT I WAS THINKING.
THAT'S NOT ALL. HE SAID HE WAS ON HIS WAY HERE.
JABBA?! COMING HERE?
YEAH, AND YOU CAN BET HE WON'T BE ALONE.
WE'VE GOT TO GET YOU OUT OF HERE!
WHAT ABOUT HIM?
GRAPH! MAW!
NO, CHEWIE! WE CAN'T KILL HIM!
YOU'RE RIGHT...
...I'VE GOT A BETTER IDEA.

LATER...
THANK YOU FOR YOUR HELP.
IT WAS MY PLEASURE, YOUR HIGHNESS.
MY CREW WASN'T ABLE TO FINISH ALL THE REPAIRS, BUT THE FALCON'S HYPER-DRIVE SHOULD BE WORKING.
THANKS, PAL. SORRY ABOUT THE DISTURBANCE.
YOU SHOULD BE. NOW GET OUTTA HERE BEFORE YOU CAUSE ANY MORE TROUBLE...

SET COURSE FOR DAGOBAH, CHEWIE.

THANKS, FELLAS!
YEAH, THIS MAKES A PERFECT DESK...
BARON CALRISSIAN?
WE'VE JUST RECEIVED A TRANSMISSION FROM A SHIP IN ORBIT FOR SOMEONE BY THE NAME OF BOBA FETT.
Hm? NO FETT HERE. TELL THEM TO GO AWAY.
Uh, THEY'RE IMPERIALS, SIR. I THINK YOU BETTER TAKE THIS ONE.
THE EMPIRE?! I THOUGHT HE WAS WORKING FOR JABBA!

BARON ADMINISTRATOR. YOU WILL PATCH ME THROUGH TO FETT IMMEDIATELY.
HE IS ON A MISSION FOR THE EMPIRE AND I WILL TOLERATE NO FURTHER DELAYS.

LORD VADER... um... FETT IS UNAVAILABLE AT THE MOMENT. Er... WHAT I MEAN TO SAY IS...

...HE LEFT UNEXPECTEDLY.
DO NOT TOY WITH ME, ADMINISTRATOR.

THE REBEL HAN SOLO AND HIS CREW WERE TRACKED TO THIS FACILITY. YOU WILL TURN THEM OVER NOW.
YOU JUST MISSED THEM. THEY LEFT RIGHT BEFORE YOU SHOWED UP?

MOST UNFORTUNATE. FETT ASSURED ME YOU WOULD DETAIN SOLO.
AS YOU HAVE NOT, I CAN ONLY ASSUME YOU CITY IS A REBEL BASE OPERATIONS AND MUST BE DESTROYED.

VROAARRR!
NO! WAIT!
ATTENTION! THIS IS ADMINISTRATOR CALRISSIAN. THE CITY IS UNDER ATTACK BY IMPERIAL FORCES. EVACUATE THE CITY IMMEDIATELY! EVACUATE!
BROOM
BADOOM
TOOOM

HURRY, EVERYONE! HURRY!

TARGET ALL TURBOLASERS ON THEIR REPULSORLIFT GENERATORS AND FIRE.

VTOOM
VTOOM
THEY'VE HIT THE REPULSORS!
KATHOOM

THOOM

MEANWHILE, NEAR DAGOBAH...
I NEVER SAW THIS COMING...
...WHO'D HAVE THOUGHT I'D BECOME A JEDI? ACTUALLY, I'M WORRIED. WHAT IF I DON'T HAVE WHAT IT TAKES?
WHAT IF IT'S ALL A MISTAKE?
CAPTAIN SOLO, PLEASE COME QUICKLY. THERE'S SOMETHING WRONG WITH MISTRESS LEIA.
I WAS OVERCOME BY TERROR, AND THEN IT DISAPPEARED-- REPLACED BY NOTHINGNESS, LIKE I WAS SURROUNDED BY A VOID...
PROBABLY JUST THE PAST FEW DAYS CATCHING UP WITH YOU...
IT'S OKAY NOW. WE'RE ALMOST TO DAGOBAH.
ONCE WE'RE THERE, YOU CAN REST.

EASY, CHEWIE. WATCH THOSE BRANCHES.
ANYONE HAVE AN IDEA WHERE WE CAN FIND THIS YODA?
SWEEP-PWOOP! REET. TWEET-BOOP. BLEEP!
ARTOO SAYS THERE ARE TOO MANY LIFE-SIGNS TO DISTINGUISH A SPECIFIC INDIVIDUAL.
HOWEVER, HE DOES SENSE WOOD-SMOKE COMING FROM FOUR HUNDRED METERS AHEAD. IT COULD BE A SETTLEMENT.
COME ON, CHEWIE. LET'S CHECK IT OUT.
WAIT! I'M COMING WITH YOU.

MAYBE YOU SHOULD STAY BACK AT THE SHIP. MY FORCE-SENSE TELLS ME THIS PLACE IS DANGEROUS.
NO, IT'S NOT. I DON'T KNOW WHY, BUT THIS PLACE SEEMS LIKE--HOME.
GRAW! MRAPH RAW GRAW!
NO, CHEWIE, I DON'T THINK SHE'S PART WOOKIEE.
LOOK. THERE...
WELCOME, FRIENDS. EXPECTING YOU, I WAS.

YODA, I AM. TRAIN YOU AS A JEDI, I WILL.
ALTHOUGH, THIS IS UNFORSEEN...
...EXPECTING A DIFFERENT SKYWALKER, I WAS.
ME?
BUT I'M NOT A SKYWALKER.
MISTAKEN, YOU ARE. I KNEW YOUR MOTHER, YOU HAVE HER EYES. SHE GAVE BIRTH TO TWINS. LUKE WAS YOUR BROTHER. STRONG IS THE FORCE WITH YOUR FAMILY. WITH YOU AND YOUR FATHER...
...DARTH VADER.

WAIT! I'M THE CHOSEN ONE! LUKE SAID I WAS SUPPOSED TO TRAIN AS A JEDI, NOT LEIA!
AND VADER'S NOT HER FATHER! THAT'S IMPOSSIBLE!
Hmph!
HOW?
YOU CAN'T DO THIS, LEIA! YOUR PLACE IS AT THE HEAD OF THE REBELLION!
THEY NEED YOU! THE POND-HOPPER HERE'S FEEDING YOU LIES!
NO, HAN. YODA'S TELLING THE TRUTH. I CAN FEEL IT. LUKE'S MESSAGE WAS FOR ME ALL ALONG. IT'S GOING TO BE OKAY.
BUT... THE REBELLION NEEDS YOU
I NEED YOU.
AND IT'S NOT SAFE HERE.
Oh, HAN...

Ehr?
SAFER WITH JEDI MASTER YODA SHE WILL BE THAN WITH A DEATH-MARKED SCOUNDREL LIKE YOU!
HEY!

HOW DO YOU KNOW ABOUT THE BOUNTY ON MY HEAD?

JEDI, I AM... REMEMBER?
NOW COME. I HAVE PREPARED FOOD.

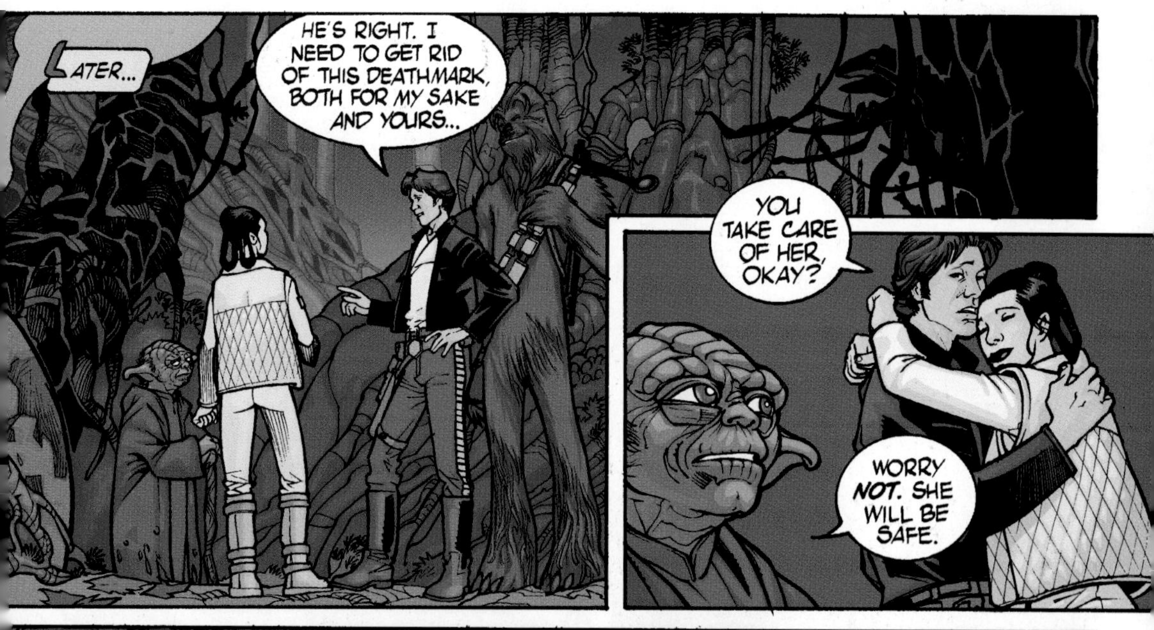
LATER...
HE'S RIGHT. I NEED TO GET RID OF THIS DEATHMARK, BOTH FOR MY SAKE AND YOURS...
YOU TAKE CARE OF HER, OKAY?
WORRY NOT. SHE WILL BE SAFE.

MUCH WE MUST DO. TRAIN HARD, YOU WILL. IT WILL BE DIFFICULT.

YOU WILL FACE DARKNESS AND TRIAL. BUT STRONG YOU MUST BE, FOR NOW ALL RESTS ON YOUR FATE.

NEXT TIME YOU SEE YOUR FRIENDS...

...A JEDI YOU WILL BE.

DAGOBAH.
MANY MONTHS LATER...
LIKE A RIVER, THE FORCE FLOWS THROUGH YOU.
LEARNED MUCH YOU HAVE, IN THESE PAST THREE MONTHS.
AND MORE QUICKLY THAN ANY STUDENT I HAVE TAUGHT BEFORE.
EVEN MY FATHER?
KZT

STRONG WAS THE FORCE WITH ANAKIN, BEFORE HE BECAME VADER.
YET IMPATIENT AND STUBBORN HE WAS. CONSTANTLY PUSHING TO EXCEL BEYOND HIS ABILITY.
KZT
SHRSH
SHH
SHRSH
MORE SUBLIME, YOUR APPROACH HAS BEEN.
REAAK!
!!

CHOMP
VMM
BAAAAAAAAAGH
PLOOSH
YET LEARNED YOU HAVE NOT THE HAZARDS OF USING A SUPER-HEATED BLADE AGAINST A FOE MADE MAINLY OF WATER...

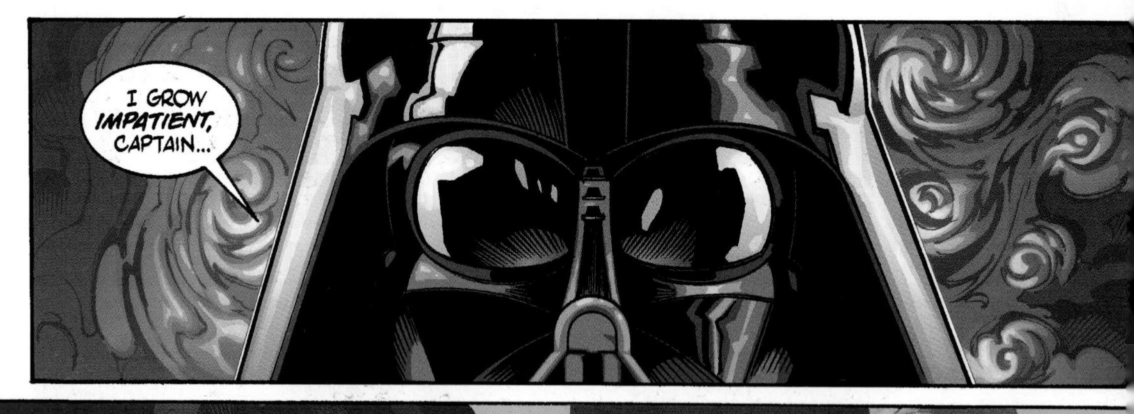
I GROW *IMPATIENT,* CAPTAIN...

YET ANOTHER DEAD END. NO SOLO AND NOT A TRACE OF SKYWALKER.
PERHAPS YOU SHOULD FOCUS YOUR EFFORTS ELSEWHERE, MY LORD.
POSSIBLY ON THE CONSTRUCTION OF THE EMPEROR'S NEW BATTLE STATION.
I HAVE HEARD RUMOR THAT SKYWALKER WAS KILLED ON HOTH--
THAT RUMOR COULD PROVE YOUR UNDOING, CAPTAIN. *SKYWALKER IS* ALIVE.

I HAVE SENSED HIS PRESENCE. HE DOES LIVE.
AFTER I FIND HIM, HE WILL JOIN ME AND TOGETHER WE SHALL DO THE EMPEROR'S BIDDING.

I SUGGEST YOU REMEMBER THAT, CAPTAIN...

I'M RETURNING TO THE EXECUTOR. INFORM THEM OF MY ARRIVAL.

LORD VADER! A FRESH SHIPMENT OF PROBE DROIDS JUST ARRIVED AND ADDITIONAL BOUNTY HUNTERS AWAIT YOUR ORDERS.
LAUNCH THE DROIDS AS SOON AS THEY'VE BEEN PROGRAMMED, AND BRIEF THE BOUNTY HUNTERS.
I SENSE MY SEARCH IS COMING TO A CLOSE.

"SOON, SKYWALKER WILL BE MINE..."

IT TOOK US LONGER THAN I THOUGHT, BUT WE DID IT. NOW ALL WE'VE GOT TO DO IS TRANSFER THE MONEY OVER TO JABBA.
GAWRPH. MWARR.

OF COURSE WE'RE NOT GONNA WALK RIGHT UP TO HIM. I ARRANGED FOR A COURIER.
AFTER ALL THIS TIME, THERE'S NO WAY I'M SETTIN' FOOT ANYWHERE NEAR JABBA...

HEY... ARE YOU GRAHRK?

PLEASE TO CALL ME UNCLE VILLIE...

Um, RIGHT, UNCLE VILLIE... I'M SOLO. YOU'LL TAKE MY MONEY TO JABBA?

ACTUALLY, IS CHANGE OF PLAN.

UNCLE VILLIE DECIDE TO SELL YOU TO JABBA INSTEAD.
OH, MY!

UNCLE VILLIE MAKE MORE MONEY THAT WAY--AND GET TO KEEP YOUR SHIP...

I'LL GET YOU, GRAHRK! WE'RE NOT FINISHED!

MASTER, VISITORS HAVE ARRIVED WITH A PLEASANT SURPRISE!
<EXCELLENT! BRING THEM TO ME...>
JABBA, LISTEN, I'VE GOT YOUR MONEY...
<HO-HO-HO! HAN, MY LONG-LOST BOY...>
<IT'S TOO LATE FOR THAT. YOU STOLE FROM ME. I CAN'T LET THAT GO UNPUNISHED.>

<TAKE THEM AWAY!>
JABBA, WAIT!
GRAWW!

GET IN THERE!
AARGH!
ZZT

I'VE GOT TO SPEAK TO JABBA! I'VE GOT HIS MONEY, I TELL YA!
GRNMPH

I REALLY MESSED UP THIS TIME, PAL...
MRAW!

"GET UP, YOU TRASH! YOU WANTED TO TALK TO JABBA? HERE'S YOUR CHANCE."

‹I WAS TOLD YOU HAD SOMETHING TO SAY TO ME, SOLO...›

JABBA! I CAN GET YOU MORE MONEY IF THAT'S WHAT YOU NEED. IT WASN'T MY FAULT I HAD TO DUMP THAT SPICE! YOU GOTTA GIVE ME ANOTHER CHANCE!

‹HAN, DON'T TAKE THIS PERSONALLY. I ALWAYS LIKED YOU, BUT BUSINESS IS BUSINESS.›
‹BESIDES, I'M BORED, AND WATCHING YOU DIE SHOULD PROVE ENTERTAINING!›

REEAAAR!

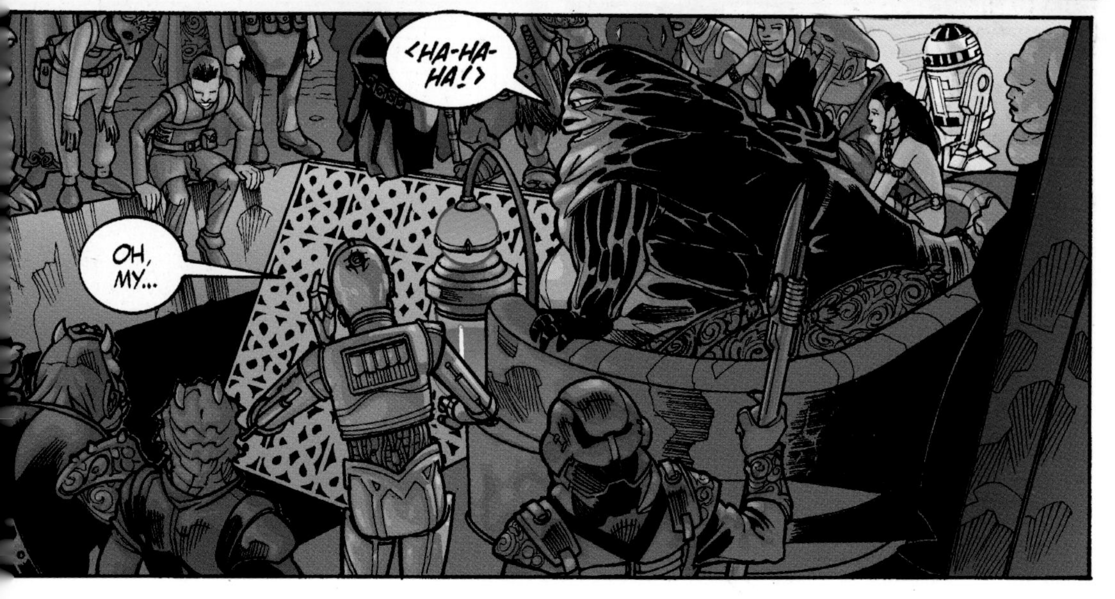

<HA-HA-HA!>
OH, MY...

GRFER!

TONK
REEES

GET 'EM!
GRAWR!

WATCH IT!
EEEEER!
click
chik

FSSH
Huh?!
BEEOWHOOP!

CHEWIE! THE DOOR!

LET'S GO!

HOMP

GAHHH!
<NO! STOP THEM! DON'T LET SOLO ESCAPE!>

:gasp!:
<THE NEXU... THEY'RE COMING FOR... US!>
RRAWR!

YEEAGH! HELP!
uh... YOU'D BETTER HURRY--JABBA NEEDS YOUR HELP!
BWOO!

GOOD GOING, ARTOO! CLOSE THE HATCH AND GET READY FOR LIFT-OFF...

GWARW. GRAAWPH RAWWP.
NO TIME TO GO BACK FOR THREEPIO NOW.
WE'LL HAVE TO TRY AND GET HIM LATER.

IT AIN'T THE *FALCON*, BUT IT'LL DO UNTIL I CAN GET THE OLD GIRL BACK.
BWOOO...

THE NEXT MORNING...

LORD VADER, WE'VE HELD THE PERIMETER SINCE BEFORE SUNRISE. NO ONE HAS LEFT THE BUILDING.

WHAT HAPPENED HERE?
WE'RE NOT SURE, SIR.

<...AND MAKE A NOTE... NO MORE ***NEXU!*** GET SOMETHING MORE CONTROLLABLE... A ***RANCOR***, PERHAPS.>

JABBA THE HUTT...
I'VE RECEIVED WORD THAT YOU ARE HOLDING HAN SOLO AND THE WOOKIEE CHEW-BACCA PRISONER. YOU WILL HAND THEM OVER TO ME.
‹SOLO?! IF I NEVER HEAR THAT NAME AGAIN, IT WILL BE TOO SOON!›

‹YOU'RE TOO LATE. SOLO AND HIS WOOKIEE ESCAPED LAST NIGHT. THEY STOLE A CARGO VESSEL AND DISAPPEARED.›
‹I DON'T KNOW WHERE THEY ARE... AND FRANKLY I HOPE TO NEVER SEE THEM AGAIN!›
Oh, MY CIRCUITS...

I AM TAKING THE DROID.

< FINE. TAKE THE DROID. IT BELONGED TO SOLO ANYWAY! GOOD RIDDANCE! >
Oh... Oh, MY...

< FORTUNA?! WHERE ARE YOU?! NOW WE NEED A NEW TRANSLATOR DROID AS WELL...! >

LORD VADER! WHERE'S SOLO? WHAT HAPPENED?
I HAVE EVERYTHING I NEED RIGHT HERE, LIEUTENANT.

DO YOU RECALL WHO BUILT YOU?
I NO LONGER HAVE THAT MEMORY, SIR. I'M AFRAID THAT INFORMATION WAS LOST LONG AGO.

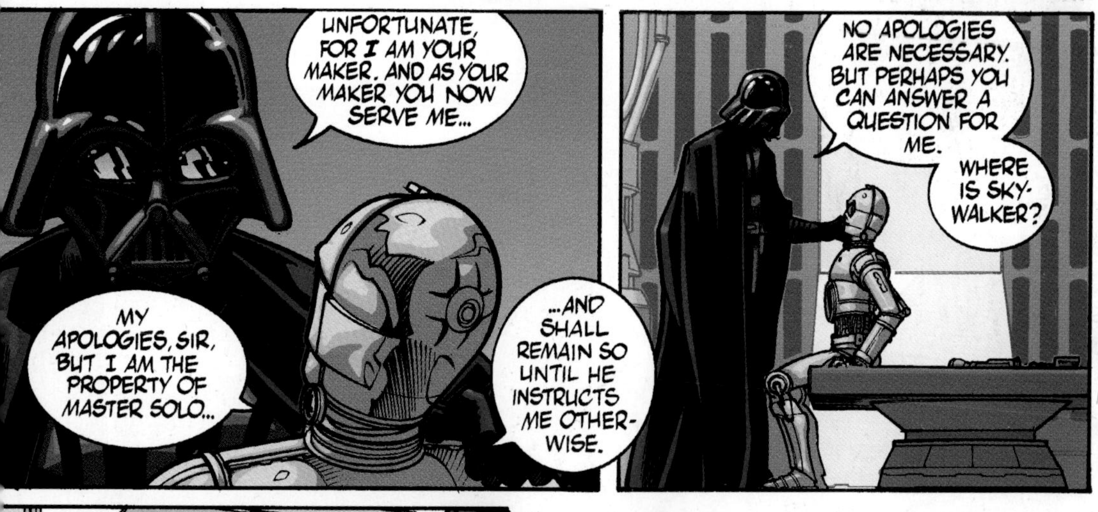
UNFORTUNATE, FOR *I* AM YOUR MAKER. AND AS YOUR MAKER YOU NOW SERVE ME...
MY APOLOGIES, SIR, BUT I AM THE PROPERTY OF MASTER SOLO...
...AND SHALL REMAIN SO UNTIL HE INSTRUCTS ME OTHERWISE.
NO APOLOGIES ARE NECESSARY. BUT PERHAPS YOU CAN ANSWER A QUESTION FOR ME.
WHERE IS SKYWALKER?

Oh, MY! I CAN'T TELL YOU THAT, SIR! IT WOULD BE AGAINST MY PROGRAMMING TO BETRAY MY MASTER OR HIS COLLEAGUES!

AS I THOUGHT. NO MATTER, THOUGH. THERE ARE OTHER WAYS OF FINDING OUT WHAT I WANT TO KNOW.
KZT

NOW, LET ME ASK YOU AGAIN. WHERE IS *SKYWALKER?*
ZZT

DZSCH DA-GO-BAH... HZZCH

COMMANDER, CHANGE COURSE AND HAVE MY SHUTTLE PREPARED. WE'RE GOING TO THE DAGOBAH SYSTEM.

DAGOBAH.
MASTER... I SEE IT...

THE CRYSTAL. FOR MY LIGHTSABER... IT'S IN A CAVE NOT FAR FROM HERE...
Hm? Er?

Ah, YES. THE CRYSTALS. SEEDED THEM I DID WHEN I FIRST CAME TO DAGOBAH.
THE HEART OF A JEDI'S WEAPON, IT IS. RETRIEVE THIS CRYSTAL YOU MUST.

NORMALLY, CONSTRUCT HER OWN HILT, A JEDI WOULD. YET SCARCE ARE SUPPLIES HERE IN THE SWAMP.
USE THIS WEAPON AND REPLACE ITS CRYSTAL WITH YOUR OWN.
ONCE I'VE COMPLETED THIS TASK, WILL I BE A JEDI?

ONE FINAL TASK, YOU WILL FACE...
...AND THEN A JEDI YOU WILL BE.

NOW GO. WITH A CLEAR MIND, FIND THE CRYSTAL, YOU WILL...
...AND RETURN BY MORNING WITH YOUR WEAPON COMPLETED.

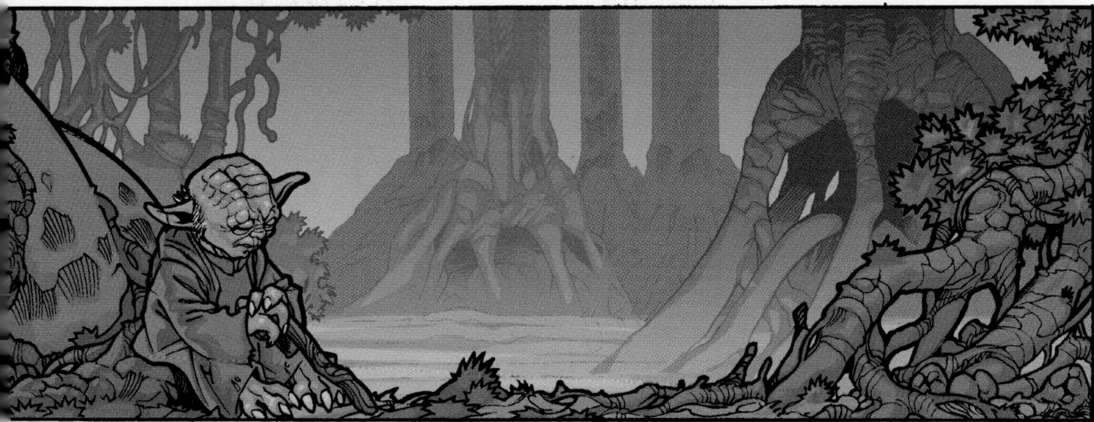

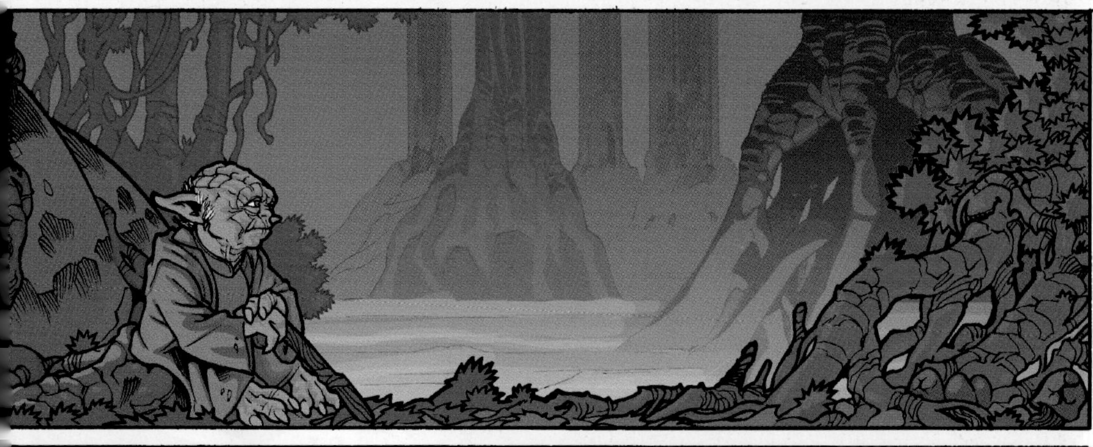

VADER. EXPECTED YOU, I HAVE...

I HAVE COME FOR MY SON, JEDI. WHERE IS HE?
SAD I AM TO SAY, FIND YOUR SON HERE, YOU WILL NOT.

DO *NOT* TOY WITH ME, JEDI.

TOO OLD AM I FOR GAMES, VADER.
YES, I AM SURPRISED TO SEE YOU'RE STILL ALIVE.

MANY SURPRISES WILL THERE BE FOR YOU THIS DAY...
KZ-VASH

WHAT? WHAT HAVE YOU DONE?

ENTERED YOUR MIND, I HAVE.
EVEN MORE TWISTED ARE YOU HERE, THAN IN THE PHYSICAL REALM.

YOUR TRICKS WILL NOT SAVE YOU, JEDI. I WILL DESTROY YOU.
KZZZT

VERY CLEVER, ELF!

BUT IT WILL TAKE MORE THAN SPECTERS TO SAVE YOU!

KZZAK

SPECTERS THEY MAY BE, YET YOUR SPECTERS THEY ARE. HURT YOU THEY CAN.

UMM

SHOOM

MY LIFE IS PAIN, JEDI. IT WILL TAKE MORE THAN THAT TO STOP ME...

MASTER!

PAIN YOUR LIFE MAY HAVE BEEN FILLED WITH, YET OF YOUR OWN CHOOSING, IT WAS.

AAGH!
ZZKT

THOOM

WRONG CHOICES YOU HAVE BEEN MAKING YOUR ENTIRE LIFE. SELFISH AND CRUEL YOU HAVE BEEN.
THINKING NEVER OF OTHERS. HIDING FROM COMPASSION. HIDING FROM THE *TRUTH!*

AND WHAT TRUTH WOULD THAT BE?

THAT *HUMAN,* YOU ARE!

CAPABLE OF LOVE. CAPABLE OF MAKING MISTAKES *AND* LEARNING FROM THEM.
FALLIBLE YOU ARE, YET DENIED THIS, YOU DID. SEEING YOURSELF ONLY AS BETTER THAN OTHERS.

UMMMM
EVEN YOUR SEARCH FOR YOUR SON, WRAPPED IN LIES IT IS.

ARG!
KZZKT
CLAIM THAT FOR YOUR EMPEROR YOU WISH TO FIND LUKE. DENYING YOUR TRUE FEELINGS TO BE A FATHER TO YOUR SON!

UNFORTUNATE, THAT YOU HAVE WASTED YOUR LIFE DEVOTED TO HATE AND LIES. HURT YOURSELF AND SO MANY OTHERS, YOU HAVE.
YEAGH!
KZZAK

ABOVE DAGOBAH...

OKAY, PAL. GET READY TO SET DOWN.
MRAWG GRAWLMPH WAAAG.

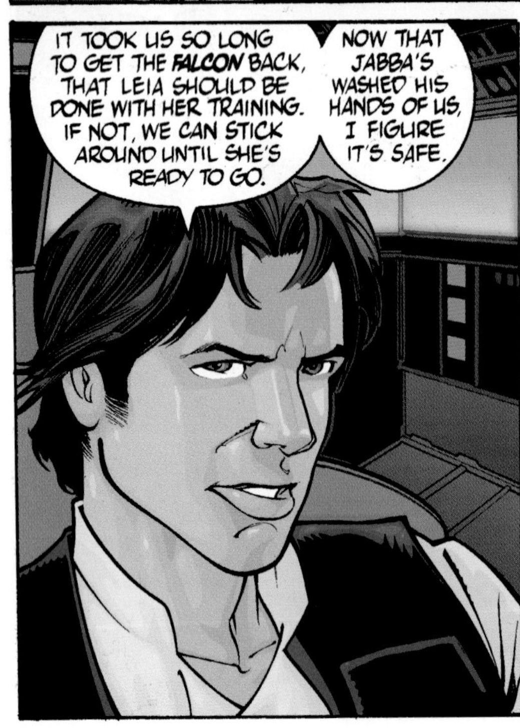
IT TOOK US SO LONG TO GET THE FALCON BACK, THAT LEIA SHOULD BE DONE WITH HER TRAINING. IF NOT, WE CAN STICK AROUND UNTIL SHE'S READY TO GO.
NOW THAT JABBA'S WASHED HIS HANDS OF US, I FIGURE IT'S SAFE.

BESIDES, I REALLY MISS HER.

ALL THIS TIME, SEARCHING IN VAIN YOU HAVE BEEN.

HUNTING THE GALAXY, WHEN ALL ALONG YOUR SON LAY BURIED IN AN ICY GRAVE. TOO LATE, YOU ARE. YOUR SON IS DEAD.

NO...

sniff
I'M... I'M SCARED...

NO LONGER DO YOU NEED TO BE AFRAID.

BUT YOU DO!

NO!

VMMMM

RAAAGH!
ZZAK

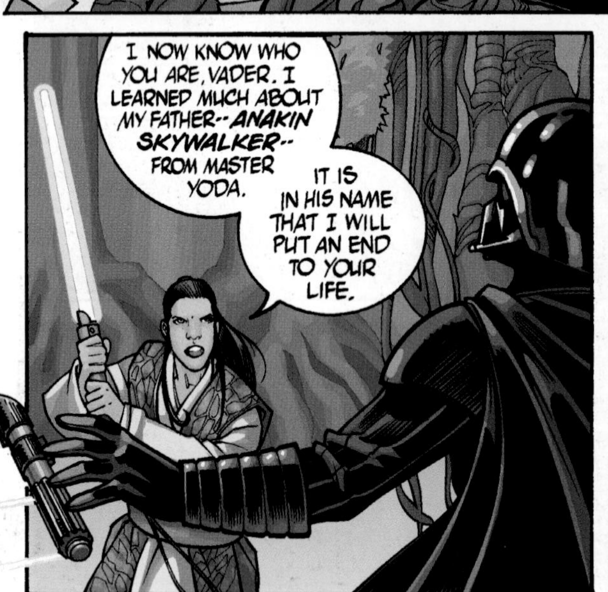
I NOW KNOW WHO YOU ARE, VADER. I LEARNED MUCH ABOUT MY FATHER-- ANAKIN SKYWALKER-- FROM MASTER YODA.
IT IS IN HIS NAME THAT I WILL PUT AN END TO YOUR LIFE.

I HAD GREAT PLANS FOR YOUR BROTHER.
THERE IS NO NEED FOR THEM TO DISAPPEAR ALONG WITH HIM.
YOU CAN JOIN ME.

I WILL NEVER JOIN YOU!

KRAK!

JOIN ME, AND WE SHALL RULE THE GALAXY TOGETHER!
I NEVER WANTED TO RULE THE GALAXY. I ONLY WANT PEACE. FATHER...
LEIA, MY CHILD... IF ONLY YOU COULD UNDER-STAND THE POWER OF THE DARK SIDE...

AGH!
VOW
VOW
LEIA! ARE YOU OKAY?!
FATHER...
I had... have... a daughter...

LEIA?
MASTER YODA?
MASTER...
Be at peace. Restored balance, you have...
Remember, you must. Find others.
Teach them as I have taught you. Triumph, you will...
...a JEDI you are...

LATER...
LEIA, I'M SORRY. I THOUGHT HE WAS GOING TO KILL YOU.
DON'T BE SORRY. PERHAPS HE WAS GOING TO KILL ME. IT DOESN'T MATTER NOW.

HE FOUND PEACE IN THE END.
I ONLY HOPE WE CAN ALL DO AS MUCH.
BUT RIGHT NOW...

...WE HAVE A GALAXY TO SAVE.

END

STAR WARS®

TIMELINE OF GRAPHIC NOVELS FROM DARK HORSE!

LD REPUBLIC ERA:
5,000—1000 YEARS BEFORE
TAR WARS: A NEW HOPE

les of the Jedi—
e Golden Age of the Sith
BN: 1-56971-229-8 $16.95

les of the Jedi—
e Fall of the Sith Empire
BN: 1-56971-320-0 $14.95

les of the Jedi—
nights of the Old Republic
BN: 1-56971-020-1 $14.95

les of the Jedi—
e Freedon Nadd Uprising
BN: 1-56971-307-3 $5.95

les of the Jedi—
rk Lords of the Sith
BN: 1-56971-095-3 $17.95

les of the Jedi—The Sith War
BN: 1-56971-173-9 $17.95

les of the Jedi—Redemption
BN: 1-56971-535-1 $14.95

di vs. Sith
BN: 1-56971-649-8 $17.95

SE OF THE EMPIRE ERA:
00-0 YEARS BEFORE
AR WARS: A NEW HOPE

e Stark Hyperspace War
N: 1-56971-985-3 $12.95

i Council—Acts of War
N: 1-56971-539-4 $12.95

lude to Rebellion
N: 1-56971-448-7 $14.95

th Maul
N: 1-56971-542-4 $12.95

sode I—The Phantom Menace
N: 1-56971-359-6 $12.95

sode I—
Phantom Menace Adventures
N: 1-56971-443-6 $12.95

go Fett
N: 1-56971-623-4 $5.95

n Wesell
N: 1-56971-624-2 $5.95

Jango Fett—Open Seasons
ISBN: 1-56971-671-4 $12.95

Outlander
ISBN: 1-56971-514-9 $14.95

Emissaries to Malastare
ISBN: 1-56971-545-9 $15.95

The Bounty Hunters
ISBN: 1-56971-467-3 $12.95

Twilight
ISBN: 1-56971-558-0 $12.95

The Hunt for Aurra Sing
ISBN: 1-56971-651-X $12.95

Darkness
ISBN: 1-56971-659-5 $12.95

Rite of Passage
ISBN: 1-59307-042-X $12.95

Honor and Duty
ISBN: 1-59307-546-4 $12.95

Episode II—Attack of the Clones
ISBN: 1-56971-609-9 $17.95

Clone Wars Volume 1—
The Defense of Kamino
ISBN: 1-56971-962-4 $14.95

Clone Wars Volume 2—
Victories and Sacrifices
ISBN: 1-56971-969-1 $14.95

Clone Wars Volume 3—
Last Stand on Jabiim
ISBN: 1-59307-006-3 $14.95

Clone Wars Volume 4—Light and Dark
ISBN: 1-59307-195-7 $16.95

Clone Wars Volume 5—The Best Blades
ISBN: 1-59307-273-2 $17.95

Clone Wars Volume 6—
On the Fields of Battle
ISBN: 1-59307-352-6 $17.95

Clone Wars Volume 7—
When They Were Brothers
ISBN: 1-59307-396-8 $17.95

Clone Wars Volume 8—
The Last Siege, The Final Truth
ISBN: 1-59307-482-4 $17.95

Clone Wars Volume 9—Endgame
ISBN: 1-59307-553-7 $17.95

Clone Wars Adventures Volume 1
ISBN: 1-59307-243-0 $6.95

Clone Wars Adventures Volume 2
ISBN: 1-59307-271-6 $6.95

Clone Wars Adventures Volume 3
ISBN: 1-59307-307-0 $6.95

Clone Wars Adventures Volume 4
ISBN: 1-59307-402-6 $6.95

Clone Wars Adventures Volume 5
ISBN: 1-59307-483-2 $6.95

Clone Wars Adventures Volume 6
ISBN: 1-59307-567-7 $6.95

Episode III—Revenge of the Sith
ISBN: 1-59307-309-7 $12.95

General Grievous
ISBN: 1-59307-442-5 $12.95

Droids—The Kalarba Adventures
ISBN: 1-56971-064-3 $17.95

Droids—Rebellion
ISBN: 1-56971-224-7 $14.95

Classic Star Wars—
Han Solo at Stars' End
ISBN: 1-56971-254-9 $6.95

Boba Fett—Enemy of the Empire
ISBN: 1-56971-407-X $12.95

Underworld—The Yavin Vassilika
ISBN: 1-56971-618-8 $15.95

Dark Forces—Soldier for the Empire
ISBN: 1-56971-348-0 $14.95

Empire Volume 1—Betrayal
ISBN: 1-56971-964-0 $12.95

Empire Volume 2—Darklighter
ISBN: 1-56971-975-6 $17.95

REBELLION ERA:
0-5 YEARS AFTER
STAR WARS: A NEW HOPE

A New Hope—The Special Edition
ISBN: 1-56971-213-1 $9.95

Empire Volume 3—
The Imperial Perspective
ISBN: 1-59307-128-0 $17.95

Empire Volume 4—
The Heart of the Rebellion
ISBN: 1-59307-308-9 $17.95

Empire Volume 5—Allies and Adversaries
ISBN: 1-59307-466-2 $14.95

A Long Time Ago... Volume 1—
Doomworld
ISBN: 1-56971-754-0 $29.95

A Long Time Ago... Volume 2—
Dark Encounters
ISBN: 1-56971-785-0 $29.95

Classic Star Wars—
The Early Adventures
ISBN: 1-56971-178-X $19.95

Classic Star Wars Volume 1—
In Deadly Pursuit
ISBN: 1-56971-109-7 $16.95

Classic Star Wars Volume 2—
The Rebel Storm
ISBN: 1-56971-106-2 $16.95

Classic Star Wars Volume 3—
Escape to Hoth
ISBN: 1-56971-093-7 $16.95

Jabba the Hutt—The Art of the Deal
ISBN: 1-56971-310-3 $9.95

Vader's Quest
ISBN: 1-56971-415-0 $11.95

Splinter of the Mind's Eye
ISBN: 1-56971-223-9 $14.95

The Empire Strikes Back—
The Special Edition
ISBN: 1-56971-234-4 $9.95

A Long Time Ago... Volume 3—
Resurrection of Evil
ISBN: 1-56971-786-9 $29.95

A Long Time Ago... Volume 4—
Screams in the Void
ISBN: 1-56971-787-7 $29.95

A Long Time Ago... Volume 5—
Fool's Bounty
ISBN: 1-56971-906-3 $29.95

Battle of the Bounty Hunters
Pop-Up Book
ISBN: 1-56971-129-1 $17.95

Shadows of the Empire
ISBN: 1-56971-183-6 $17.95

Return of the Jedi—The Special Edition
ISBN: 1-56971-235-2 $9.95

A Long Time Ago... Volume 6—
Wookiee World
ISBN: 1-56971-907-1 $29.95

A Long Time Ago... Volume 7—
Far, Far Away
ISBN: 1-56971-908-X $29.95

Mara Jade—By the Emperor's Hand
ISBN: 1-56971-401-0 $15.95

Shadows of the Empire: Evolution
ISBN: 1-56971-441-X $14.95

NEW REPUBLIC ERA:
5-25 YEARS AFTER
STAR WARS: A NEW HOPE

Omnibus—X-Wing Rogue Squadron
Volume 1
ISBN: 1-59307-572-3 $24.95

X-Wing Rogue Squadron—
Battleground Tatooine
ISBN: 1-56971-276-X $12.95

X-Wing Rogue Squadron—
The Warrior Princess
ISBN: 1-56971-330-8 $12.95

X-Wing Rogue Squadron—
Requiem for a Rogue
ISBN: 1-56971-331-6 $12.95

X-Wing Rogue Squadron—
In the Empire's Service
ISBN: 1-56971-383-9 $12.95

X-Wing Rogue Squadron—
Blood and Honor
ISBN: 1-56971-387-1 $12.95

X-Wing Rogue Squadron—
Masquerade
ISBN: 1-56971-487-8 $12.95

X-Wing Rogue Squadron—
Mandatory Retirement
ISBN: 1-56971-492-4 $12.95

Dark Forces—Rebel Agent
ISBN: 1-56971-400-2 $14.95

Dark Forces—Jedi Knight
ISBN: 1-56971-433-9 $14.95

Heir to the Empire
ISBN: 1-56971-202-6 $19.95

Dark Force Rising
ISBN: 1-56971-269-7 $17.95

The Last Command
ISBN: 1-56971-378-2 $17.95

Boba Fett—
Death, Lies, and Treachery
ISBN: 1-56971-311-1 $12.95

Dark Empire
ISBN: 1-59307-039-X $16.95

Dark Empire II
ISBN: 1-59307-526-X $19.95

Empire's End
ISBN: 1-56971-306-5 $5.95

Crimson Empire
ISBN: 1-56971-355-3 $17.95

Crimson Empire II: Council of Blood
ISBN: 1-56971-410-X $17.95

Jedi Academy: Leviathan
ISBN: 1-56971-456-8 $11.95

Union
ISBN: 1-56971-464-9 $12.95

NEW JEDI ORDER ERA:
25+ YEARS AFTER
STAR WARS: A NEW HOPE

Chewbacca
ISBN: 1-56971-515-7 $12.95

INFINITIES:
DOES NOT APPLY TO TIMELINE

Infinites: A New Hope
ISBN: 1-56971-648-X $12.95

Infinities: The Empire Strikes Back
ISBN: 1-56971-904-7 $12.95

Infinities: Return of the Jedi
ISBN: 1-59307-206-6 $12.95

Star Wars Tales Volume 1
ISBN: 1-56971-619-6 $19.95

Star Wars Tales Volume 2
ISBN: 1-56971-757-5 $19.95

Star Wars Tales Volume 3
ISBN: 1-56971-836-9 $19.95

Star Wars Tales Volume 4
ISBN: 1-56971-989-6 $19.95

Star Wars Tales Volume 5
ISBN: 1-59307-286-4 $19.95

Star Wars Tales Volume 6
ISBN: 1-59307-447-6 $19.95

FOR MORE INFORMATION ABOUT THESE BOOKS VISIT DARKHORSE.COM!

AVAILABLE AT YOUR LOCAL COMICS SHOP OR BOOKSTORE

To find a comics shop in your area, call 1-888-266-4226. For more information or to order direct, visit darkhorse.com or call 1-800-862-0052 Mon.–Fri. 9 A.M. to 5 P.M. Pacific Time. *Prices and availability subject to change without notice.